The Woodcarver's Daughter

The Woodcarver's Daughter

Yona Zeldis McDonough

KAR-BEN
PUBLISHING

KAR-BEN PUBLISHING®
An imprint of Lerner Publishing Group, Inc.
241 First Avenue North
Minneapolis, MN 55401 USA

Website address: www.karben.com

Cover and interior illustrations by Kaja Kajfez.

Background: Tamara Kulikova/Shutterstock.com.

Main body text set in Bembo Std.
Typeface provided by Monotype Typography.

Library of Congress Cataloging-in-Publication Data

Names: McDonough, Yona Zeldis, author. | Kajfez, Kaja, illustrator.
Title: The woodcarver's daughter / Yona Zeldis McDonough ; [illustrated by Kaja
    Kajfez].
Description: Minneapolis : Kar-Ben Publishing, [2021] | Audience: Ages 8–11. |
    Audience: Grades 4–6. | Summary: "When a pogrom forces Batya's Russian
    Jewish family to leave their home for America, Batya hopes her new life will
    give her a chance to become a woodcarver like her father" —Provided by
    publisher
Identifiers: LCCN 2019056349 | ISBN 9781541586673
Subjects: CYAC: Immigrants—Fiction. | Wood carvers—Fiction. | Sex role—
    Fiction. | Jews—United States—Fiction. | Russian Americans—Fiction. |
    New York (N.Y.)—History—1898-1951—Fiction.
Classification: LCC PZ7.M15655 Wo 2021 | DDC [Fic]—dc23

LC record available at https://lccn.loc.gov/2019056349

Manufactured in the United States of America
1-47380-48001-6/16/2020

For Susanna Einstein,
agent extraordinaire
—Y.Z.M.

Chapter 1
Sugar

The sky is still dark when I go to the window. No light can be seen through the slats in the wooden shutters, and I carefully pull one back, hoping the slow *c-r-e-a-k* won't wake anyone else in the cottage. I crane my neck to peer up at the sky. It's dark, but clear. No clouds at all. I keep staring, as if my fierce gaze will keep the clouds—and the rain—away.

I pull my head back inside. My parents are asleep in their bed way over by the far wall. The beds of my sisters, Gittel and Sarah, are closer, so I can make out their forms. Sarah is curled up on her side like a little mouse. Gittel sleeps like a lady, hands placed neatly outside the covers, mouth closed. Avram, my older brother, is rest-less in sleep. And he snores!

But I'm too excited to sleep. Today is my twelfth birthday. And today is the day Papa has promised to take us to the fair. I'm so happy that I'll get to go. Last year there was a big storm, and the fair was called off. Two years ago I was sick, and the year before that, Papa didn't have the money to take us. So I've been praying that this year, nothing will go wrong.

I know all about the fair. It has a fortune-teller, a puppet theater, and real live dancing bears. And the things you can buy! A lace-edged handkerchief, a toy drum, a doll with a felt dress. Then there's the food—blini, pierogi, roasted nuts, and gingerbread.

The sky is brighter now. I get dressed so I can do my chores. Even though it's a special day, I still have to feed the chickens, gather the eggs, and milk the cow. And I must give oats and fresh water to Mala, the little black horse that I love almost as much as I love my Mama and Papa. Mala is high-strung and spirited. She knocks her bucket of oats all over the stall floor. When

Avram tries to ride her, she throws him off. Oh, she's a naughty one! Papa keeps threatening to sell her, but I don't think he will. Deep down, he loves her too.

* * *

An hour later, we're seated in our wooden cart, on our way. Mala's black coat shines in the morning light, and she holds her head high. On one side of me is Sarah, who is only four. She bounces up and down on the seat while Gittel, who is a year younger than me but who acts two years older, sits primly, hands folded in her lap. Avram is asleep. His mouth is open, and he's snoring—again!

"Sarah, stop," says Gittel crossly. "You're on my skirt."

"She's excited—can't you see?" I say.

"Well, you may not care if your apron is stained or your hair is snarled. But I do!"

I look down to see that, yes, there is a yellow smear on my apron. And in my rush to get ready, I didn't do a very good job fixing my hair.

"Some people have more important things to do than to fuss over their clothes!"

"No fighting," says Mama. She turns to Sarah. "You'll wear yourself out before we get there. Settle down."

"All right." Sarah is briefly still, but as soon as Mama turns, she starts bouncing again. Avram stirs, and his butter-blond curls fall across his face. Gittel and I envy those curls. But I envy a lot of things about Avram, not just his hair.

I decide to ignore Gittel and Avram and look at the scenery. We go past the woods and onto the open road. Soon I see the cottages and the wooden *shul* of the next village, and next, there is a long stretch filled only with fields and sky. Mala keeps up a lively pace—*clip CLOP, clip CLOP*—and soon we're on the outskirts of the town. "We're almost there," I announce. And although I don't bounce, I'm as excited as Sarah.

Sarah's jostling wakes Avram, who rubs his eyes and mumbles, "Almost where?"

"The fair, you silly!" cries Sarah.

"My skirt!" Gittel says, smoothing the cotton with her hand.

Gittel and her stupid old skirt, I think. I give Sarah's shoulders a little squeeze.

"Girls, what did I say about quarreling?" Mama asks. But she's smiling. Mama, like the rest of us, is looking forward to the fair. Papa clucks his tongue to tell Mala to stop, and then he gets down to tie her up. We're here!

◆ ◆ ◆

I've been to town before on market days with Papa. I've seen the stalls crammed with cherries, plums splitting their skins, currants in their wicker baskets. I remember the butcher and the fishmonger and the baker with his loaves piled way up high. There was a woman who sold fabric, the coiled bolts standing straight as young trees, and another who sold used shoes and boots, all heaped together—you had to dig to find a pair in your size.

But I've never been here on the day of the fair, and I can't get over how different everything looks. Garlands of evergreen boughs and flowers hang from the buildings. The stalls—so many more than on market day—are decorated with shiny fabric and still more flowers. I spy the fortune-teller with her heavy silver earrings and her silk scarf tied tightly over her black hair. She sits at a table behind a crystal ball. Right in front of her is a troupe of jugglers. One juggles apples, and another, golden hoops. A third juggles lighted torches. The crowd gasps as the torches rise and fall in the air. But the fire frightens me. Last summer, our neighbor's cottage burned down. I can still remember the way the flames gobbled up the little house, leaving only chunks of blackened wood and ashes behind.

I'd much rather look at the fortune-teller with her spangled shawl. Or the man next to her, selling round cakes that are fried in oil and sprinkled with sugar. Next to him is another man selling strawberries topped with cream.

"Papa, I want strawberries," says Sarah. "Please, can I have some?"

"And I want a fried cake," Avram adds. "Maybe two. They're small."

"Each of you can choose a treat," Papa says, reaching in his pocket for the flannel sack that holds the kopecks we can spend today. Sarah and Gittel choose the berries, and Avram picks the fried cakes.

"What about you, Batya?" Papa asks. "Wouldn't you like something too?"

I can't decide. The cakes smell delicious, and the berries look juicy and sweet. But I want something even more special. "I'll wait, Papa," I say, and we continue on our way. Here is the man with the roasted nuts; there is the gingerbread lady. I see people eating pierogi and blini. But still I don't ask for anything.

We stop at the puppet theater. I laugh at the jester's tricks and admire the princess's velvet dress. But when I glance over at Papa, I see that he is not watching the puppets. He's talking to someone; I recognize Mr. Moskowitz from the shop where Papa works as a woodcarver. Mr. Moskowitz has a merry face with blue eyes and a black beard. But today he looks worried. And so does Papa. I move closer, trying to hear what they're saying.

". . . setting houses on fire," says Mr. Moskowitz. Fires? Where? But the puppet show is over and the applause drowns out the rest of his words. Mr. Moskowitz shakes Papa's hand and says goodbye. Papa still looks worried. Is it about the fires?

I want to find out—but wait, what's this? I hear a very noisy machine and see a man standing behind it. The machine is spinning sugar into a pink cloud. It looks so light and fluffy. "Fairy floss!" calls the man. "Only two kopecks for a stick. Step right up, and try it yourself!" A crowd gathers.

"Fairy floss," repeats Sarah. "What's that?"

"It's candy," Gittel declares as if she knows everything. I stare at the man and his long paper tube. Every time it travels around the bowl of the machine, more of the floss sticks to it. Soon there's a pink, shimmery cloud of candy attached to the paper. When he removes it from the machine, the sugary crystals glint in the sun. I have to try it. "Papa, can I have a stick of fairy floss?"

"It's two kopecks," Papa says. He worries a lot about money. But then he smiles. "All right. You'll give your sisters and brother a taste, right?"

"Oh yes!" I say, though I wish I didn't have to share with Gittel. Papa tells the man to prepare another stick, and I watch as he spins a new pink cloud and hands it to me. I raise the candy to my lips. Sweet, light, and gone in an instant, it really *does* taste like something a fairy would eat. Mmm!

"Save some for me!" Sarah says, and so I hand the fluffy stick to her. She passes it to Gittel, who then gives it to Avram. After the floss is gone, Avram wants to stop at the stall where you can shoot an arrow at a target for a prize, and Sarah wants to see the bears. While they're arguing, I move closer to Papa.

"What did you and Mr. Moskowitz talk about?" I ask quietly.

"Shoptalk," Papa says. "Nothing too exciting."

"But you looked so worried," I say.

Papa stares at me as if he's trying to decide whether to say more. But before he can answer, we're interrupted, this time by the sound of music.

"What's that?" Gittel asks.

"It must be the carousel," Mama says.

"I've never seen a carousel," Avram says.

"Me neither," says Sarah.

"Let's go!" Gittel says. "We don't want to miss *that*."

Again, I forget about Papa and Mr. Moskowitz as I take my sisters' hands and hurry toward the sound. There is a crowd in front of me, so I have to wriggle my way between a man smoking a pipe and a tall woman in a dark blue dress. Finally, I reach the front—and there it is! Under the red-and-white striped awning are the leaping painted horses, spinning around in a circle. Some are black, like Mala. Others are gray, and others all the shades of brown: honey, nutmeg, cinnamon, chocolate. Their saddles are scarlet, midnight blue, gold, and green.

I move still closer so I can see their faces. They look so real! There's one that's jet black, just like Mala. Her bridle is pink, and there is a real, pale pink ostrich feather attached to her forehead.

"How beautiful!" murmurs Mama.

"And such fine workmanship!" Papa notices such things. So do I.

"Can we have a ride, Papa?" cries Sarah. "Please?"

Papa fishes out the kopecks for the tickets. Sarah, Gittel, and even Avram line up immediately. Only I hang back.

"Don't you want a ride too, *katzeleh?*" Papa says, using his favorite nickname for me, *little cat.*

"Not yet," I say. Of course I want to ride the carousel. But I have to look at it—really look—first. Each horse looks so different. The person who made these horses is more than a carver. He is an artist.

When I finally do take my ride, I climb on the black horse with the pink plume. The carousel begins to move, and everything goes by in a blur. But all too soon, the music slows, and we come to a stop. I get down, and even though it's silly, I pat the horse's muzzle. If I could, I would ride her all day.

Later, we sit on benches in the town square and eat the supper Mama has brought: black bread, boiled potatoes, cucumbers, cheese, and tart green apples. And later still, we watch a display of fireworks, the night sky exploding with color. The fireworks are pretty, but my mind keeps going back to the carousel. In my imagination, I hear the music, and I climb on top of my black horse—for she *is* mine, at least in my dreams—as she bobs up and down, up and down, up and up and up.

Chapter 2
Wood

In the morning, I'm so tired. The sky gets
lighter, and still I burrow under the covers. But
when I hear the clucking of the chickens, the
mooing of the cow, and Mala's irritated neigh-
ing, I get up and pull my clothes on in a rush.
I see that the stain is still on my apron. No time
to do anything about it now.

I race through my chores, always a step
behind. It isn't until noon that I'm finally able to
stop for a rest. And when I do, I know just where
to go. I slip quietly out the back door and hurry
along the path at the side of the cottage, passing
a big field, two more cottages, and then another
field. Next comes the shul, and after that, the

brook. I follow it until I come to the place.

I stop outside the door, trying to peek in without being seen. The floor is littered with wood: shavings, blocks, and piles of sawdust, fine as sand. There is Papa in his leather apron, head down as he carves. He doesn't notice me, which is fine, since I'm not supposed to be here anyway. Next to Papa is Avram, acting bored. Avram is fourteen, and lucky enough to be apprenticed to Papa, but does he appreciate it? He does not. Look at him now, eyes wandering all over the place, hardly paying attention.

If only we could change places! If I were the apprentice, I wouldn't just sit there like a lump, daydreaming instead of working. I would be carving, smoothing, sanding, refining. I would be learning every minute, making things with my own two hands, not looking out the window counting the dust motes or whatever it is that Avram is doing.

"Batya! What are you doing there?" booms Mr. Moskowitz. Guiltily, I step back. I think of how worried he looked at the fair, but now he seems like his usual cheery self. Still, I wish

I knew what he and Papa were talking about yesterday.

"I was just looking . . ." My voice trails off.

"Well, you can come in," he says. "You know your way around."

It's true. I do know my way around the shop—the benches and tables, the heavy planks of wood piled against the walls, the big windows streaked with sawdust—because I come here whenever I can.

Mr. Moskowitz steps back inside, and I follow. Papa sees me now and smiles.

Avram looks over too. "Is it time for lunch already?" he asks. I can tell he hopes the answer is yes.

"It is," I say, thankful he's given me an excuse to be here. I should be at home, helping to get the meal ready. Mama must be wondering where I am. But just look at what Papa is making! A piece of wood with carved openwork as delicate as lace. Scalloped edges form a border; tiny openings in the shape of crescent moons fill the rest of it.

"What is it?" I ask.

"It's for the count. Do you like it?"

"Oh yes!" I say. The count owns the finest house in town. It's very grand, with big steps leading up to a pair of oak doors that were carved in this very shop. Although I've never been inside, I've heard about the marble floors, the crystal chandeliers, the gilt-framed mirrors, and the sofas covered in fancy brocade.

"There'll be a whole row of these all across the wall," continues Papa.

"How beautiful they'll be," I say.

"Yes, they certainly will," says Mr. Moskowitz, who has come up right behind me. "The count's daughter will sleep in that room." He ruffles my hair, making it even messier than it already was. "Would you like to sleep there?" asks Mr. Moskowitz teasingly. I smile. Yes, I would. But what I want even more is to carve a piece of the room's decoration, to *make* an object like the one Papa is making, not just own it. Papa makes all sorts of beautiful objects out of wood. He carved the arks—for holding the Torah—that are used in our shul and the shuls in the nearby villages. He also carved the bimahs—the altars at which the Torah is read—and the benches where people sit.

Taking out his handkerchief, Papa wipes his face. "Let's go," he says. Avram runs ahead, picking up stones that he pitches into the brook. *Pling, pling, pling* go the stones as they hit the water.

I can hear birds overhead and the buzz of a bumblebee nearby. Wildflowers dot the side of the path, and mushrooms sprout under the trees. Sometimes, Gittel, Sarah, and I take a basket and go hunting for them. When the basket is full, we take it to Mama, who cooks the mushrooms into a tasty soup.

"Did you tell your mother where you were going?" asks Papa after we've walked in silence for a few minutes.

"Not exactly . . ." I say.

"Mmm," is all Papa says.

"She doesn't want me coming to the shop, Papa. But I can't help myself."

Papa is quiet. He knows how much I want to be a woodcarver—knows and can do nothing about it. Only boys can join the woodworkers' guild. That's why Avram was admitted two years ago. Now he works with Papa three days a week. The other three, he goes to cheder—school—another place where only boys are allowed. I want to go to school, but I want to be a carver even more. And though both Papa and Mr. Moskowitz have asked if an exception could be made for me, the answer is always no.

But I would be such a good carver! Oh, I help with the housework because girls are supposed to, but I'm no good at it. Already Gittel is so much better. Her stitches run in a straight line. She can bake challah as light as air. No one expects much from Sarah yet, but she's so lively and sweet that she brightens all our days.

But what about me? There is nothing special about me. Sometimes, I climb on Mala's shiny black back and ride her around the meadow. Riding helps me sort out my thoughts. Papa worries that I'll be thrown, but I know Mala won't throw me.

"Mama needs your help," Papa says as the cottage comes into view.

"I know, Papa," I say. "I'll try harder."

"Then you'll succeed," says Papa gently. "I have faith in you, Batya."

I stand still for a moment, taking in his praise. But I have to ask, "Papa, why won't you tell me what you and Mr. Moskowitz were talking about at the fair? It's something bad, isn't it?"

"What makes you think that?" he says.

"Because you won't say what it is."

"I don't want to worry you, katzeleh."

"But I'm more worried *not* knowing," I tell him.

He is quiet for a moment. "There've been rumors," he says finally. "About a pogrom."

I've heard about pogroms, nights of violence when drunken soldiers and peasants storm through Jewish shtetls, destroying anything and anyone they please. I know that there are many soldiers stationed in the village. Russia has been at war with Germany and Austria since 1914—a whole year. I've gotten used to seeing the soldiers. And there hasn't been a pogrom here in a long time.

"Do you really think that's true?" I say.

"I'm not sure," admits Papa, which is much less reassuring than a simple *no*.

Before I can ask anything else, I see Sarah in front of the cottage, about to pounce on one of the hens, and I catch her just in time. Good thing too; those hens have sharp beaks! When I turn back, Papa has gone inside.

I follow, leading Sarah by the hand. Avram and Gittel are already seated at the table, and Mama is serving the food.

"There you are!" she says. "I was calling and calling."

"Sorry, Mama." I start tearing off hunks of bread, putting one at each place, while Mama spoons beets, potatoes, and dumplings onto the plates. Papa says a short prayer before we begin to eat. After lunch, Papa and Avram go back to work. I stay behind to wash the dishes, sweep, and put Sarah down for a nap. When she's asleep, I step outside. Mama and Gittel are at the brook, pounding the clothes clean with big rocks, and I am alone. Finally.

I pull out the small pocketknife I always carry, along with a piece of wood. Sitting down by the side of the cottage, I begin to whittle. I love the feel of the wood in my hand growing smaller—yet more alive—as I work. Right now, I'm carving a fish, using the sharp silver blade to shape the fins, the mouth, and the round, flat eye. As I carve, I think about the pogrom. Will it happen here? I don't know; neither does Papa. But the movement of my hands calms my fears. Soon, I hear Mama and Gittel returning from the brook. Inside, Sarah is stirring. I get up. The fish still looks so rough. Why can't I join the guild and apprentice to Papa so I can really learn to carve?

"Batya?" calls Mama. "I need your help with the baskets—they're so heavy!" Stuffing the fish and the knife back in my pocket, I head down the path to help my mother.

Chapter 3
Fire

The next day, Papa and Avram leave for the shop at the usual time, but they're home before lunch, just as we've finished making jam.

"Is something wrong?" asks Mama. I look at Papa. He's red-faced and out of breath. I follow Mama and Papa outside and see the reason: There are several rough planks of wood leaning against the wall of the cottage.

"What are those doing here? Did you bring them from the shop?" I ask. Mama doesn't say anything, but her bottom lip begins to tremble.

"Pogrom," says Papa in a strained voice. "That's what they're saying down at the shop."

"When?" Mama asks. The trembling is worse now.

"Tonight," says Papa. "Mr. Moskowitz heard a rumor the other day. Today he found out for sure. He sent us all home to get ready." Papa gestures to the planks. "He gave us the wood. I wish it were more. But we had to share."

"Will they come here?" I ask. Our cottage is some distance from the other cottages in the village.

"I don't know," Papa says. "We can only pray that they won't. But in any case, we have to protect ourselves."

A pogrom! Coming here, to our little village! I'm so frightened that I can't say another word. It's like the time when Avram dared me to jump from the roof of the cottage. I landed with a terrible thud on the dirt below, not really hurt but with all the wind knocked out of me. I hadn't been able to speak for an hour. That's how I feel now.

Papa and Avram pound the boards across the windows and the door. Next, they drag our biggest pieces of furniture in front of them. Mama and Gittel cook and get food ready for later on. Mama can't risk cooking tonight, when the smoke coming up from the chimney would show that we're home. I help by keeping Sarah quiet and out of the way.

The light lingers in the sky for a long time, but finally, it's dark. We eat our supper of mashed lentils and carrots quickly and in silence. Afterward, we sit quietly in the center of the room. At first, Sarah thinks it's fun. She tries to get my attention, then Avram's, and then Gittel's. But Mama is constantly shushing her, and Sarah can't understand why.

"Let's light the fire," Sarah says. "I'm tired of sitting in the dark."

"It's too dangerous," says Papa.

"But why?" Sarah whines.

"Because Papa says so!" Mama is never this sharp. She must be very frightened.

"Come sit on my lap," I tell Sarah, and she climbs onto me. "Do you want to hear a story? I'll whisper it in your ear." If we could light a candle, I'd read her a story from the Bible we own. But we can't take the risk, so I will have to make something up.

"Yes, a story," Sarah says, settling herself. So I tell her a story about a princess who lives in the forest whose clothes are made of bark and whose crown is the cap of an acorn. She wears a necklace made of tiny berries and sleeps on a bed made of feathers dropped by the whitest, softest doves. Sarah drinks in every word.

Gittel and Avram stretch out awkwardly on the floor. We have blankets but no mattresses; the mattresses, like the pine cupboard and sideboard, are stacked in front of the windows and door. Still, a blanket is better than nothing. I wish I could stretch out too—my legs are tingling from the weight of Sarah's body. But if I make Sarah move, she might start whining again. So I force myself to be strong.

"I don't hear anything," says Gittel. "Maybe they won't come here after all. Maybe they'll all just go away."

Avram drifts off to sleep first, then Gittel, then Sarah. Even Mama's eyelids begin to close. I gently shift Sarah to the floor once she's dozed off. Now Papa and I are the only ones awake. I stretch out my legs in the dark. But just like the morning of the fair, I can't sleep. This time, it's fear, not excitement, that keeps me alert.

My eyes have adjusted to the dark, so I try to calm myself by looking around the familiar room. There is the table, carved by Papa, where we eat our meals. There is the fireplace with logs and kindling neatly stacked beside it. There is the samovar that Mama uses for making tea.

So far, nothing has happened. Maybe the rumors are false. I strain to listen but hear only the usual night noises: an owl's soft hoot, the bark of a neighbor's dog, the wind rustling in the trees. Mala is out there too; I can hear her snort and shift around in her stall.

But now—a distant thumping, soft and low at first, growing louder, more urgent. The sound of horses' hooves, thundering as they strike. I can hear voices too. Shouting. A muffled scream. And a horrible, bitter smell—something is burning.

I am more terrified than I have ever been in my life, but I do not utter a sound.

Even though the night is mild, I feel cold all over. Papa's hand reaches for mine, and I grip it tightly. The voices are loud now—loud and angry. There is laughter, but it sounds cruel. And there is cursing too. Even the horses sound angry, their neighs high-pitched and fierce. Does Mala hear them? Is she as frightened as I am? The throbbing of my heart keeps time with the hooves: *ka thump, ka thump, KA THUMP.* Louder and louder, until I think they will burst through the door in the next second. Mama is awake now. But my sisters and brother sleep on. I squeeze Papa's hand even more tightly; it is as cold as my own.

Amazingly, the sound of the hooves gets softer. At least that's what I think. With every ounce of concentration I have, I strain to hear. Yes, I'm right. The hoofbeats are fainter now. The angry horses are going away. The voices grow fainter too until I can't hear them anymore. What I do hear is a deep sigh coming from Papa. But we're still too afraid to speak, and so we sit there silently until the sky gets light.

Papa gets up, moves the furniture away from the door, and pries off the boards. Cautiously, he opens the door and looks out. The sun is hidden behind some puffy, gray clouds; there will be rain today. Everything looks fine. Our cottage is unharmed; the chickens scratch happily in the dirt. I run to the barn to see Mala. She pokes her black head out of her stall and whinnies happily.

"I'm going to the shop," Papa announces. I let my arms slide down from Mala's neck and turn to look at him.

"Do you have to?" Mama asks in a worried tone.

"Yes," he says. "Who knows what could have happened last night? I've got to find out." He rubs his hands over his face. "Maybe someone will need our help. I should be there."

"Be careful, then," says Mama.

"Can I come with you?" I ask.

"Better not," he says. "Avram will come. You stay here."

"All right, Papa," I say. "I'll stay with Mama."

"You're such a help with Sarah," Mama adds.

Her words make me feel good. There *is* something I can do besides whittle. I spend the morning with Sarah, teaching her to shell peas and fold clothes. She likes doing the peas, especially when they pop out of their pods and go rolling all over. But she's too impatient to fold clothes. "Not like that," I tell her. "See, you have to line this edge up with this edge." I smooth the pillowcase down the middle, to show her. Sarah watches for a few seconds before grabbing the pillowcase and darting off.

"Catch me, Batya!" she cries. She runs around the room, waving the pillowcase. I've just about got her cornered when she climbs over the window ledge and hops out. Now I'll have to go and find her.

But suddenly, Papa pushes the door open with such force that the knob slams the inside wall. He's always so gentle, so calm. What's come over him?

Avram trails behind him, eyes wide.

"Where's your mother?" Papa barks. His hair is even messier than mine, and his eyes are wide with alarm. Gray smudges dot his cheeks, and his clothes are covered in ash.

"She's out with the chickens—"

"Then get her! Now!"

I run out the door just as Mama is coming in; we bump into each other before Mama steps aside, staring at Papa.

"What is it?" Mama's voice is low and filled with dread. "What's happened?"

"The shop!" Papa croaks. He draws in several deep breaths, as if he can't get enough air. "The shop is gone!"

"Gone?"

"It was set on fire last night. It burned down to the ground!" Papa puts his hands to his face and lets out a harsh, terrible noise.

It takes me several seconds to understand that he is crying. I've never seen him cry before.

"What will happen to us, Papa?" I ask in a quivering voice. "And what will happen to Mr. Moskowitz?"

Papa looks up. "Mr. Moskowitz was hurt last night. In the fire."

I watch, horrified, as Papa continues to cry. Mama puts her arms around Papa. Her face is as pale as her best white linen tablecloth. But her touch must be comforting, because he lifts his face again.

"Start packing," he says. "We're leaving." His voice, though hoarse, is firm.

"But where are we going?" I ask.

"To America," Papa says. "As soon as we can."

"Who's going to America?" says Gittel, coming into the cottage. No one answers.

America! Yes, of course we know of people who have gone, driven out by worry and fear. But the idea of leaving our home, traveling all that way across the ocean—Papa might as well have asked us to climb on the backs of the honking geese and fly all the way to the moon.

The silence stretches as we all stare at Papa— until, quite abruptly, he turns and leaves the cottage, the door banging behind him.

Seconds later, Sarah comes in, pillowcase now dangling limp in her hand. "I was waiting," she says. "You didn't come."

"Oh, Sarah," I say, taking her in my arms. "I'm so sorry."

Chapter 4
Water

Of course it isn't so easy to just get up and go to America. There are things that have to be done first. There is the matter of something called papers, which Papa has to fill out three separate times. It takes him hours: scratching away with his pen, dribbling the ink, and leaving his dark fingerprints all over. When the papers are finally done, he has to deliver them to an office several villages away. He's gone for two days, and Mama is worried the whole time. But finally, Papa comes back, the papers now signed and stamped with big blobs of red sealing wax.

Next, Papa has to get the tickets, which cost a lot of money. Mama scours the cottage for things we can sell: six silver spoons that belonged to her mother, her necklace of crystal beads, our Bible with its leather cover. Papa sells them all. Finally, there is enough money to buy the tickets.

We begin to pack. Mama fills boxes with linens, dishes, and clothes. There is a special box for the samovar and one for the brass candlesticks we use on Shabbos. Still other boxes hold pots, a kettle, all the cutlery, and Papa's wood carving tools—at least the ones that weren't destroyed by the fire. Sarah wants to take a wooden doll and a cradle Papa has carved for her, and Gittel wants to take her sewing box, knitting needles, and yarn. I want my carving knife and enough wood to last the journey. Avram, standing out in front of the cottage, says he wants to take the meadow, the forest, and the brook. I know what he means. So many things have to be left behind.

"Is America far?" asks Gittel.

"Very far," says Papa.

"Will we ever come back here?" Sarah wants to know.

"No," says Papa. "We won't."

"Never?" I ask.

"Never," Papa declares.

"Can't we just move to another village?" I ask.

"What for?" says Papa angrily. "The pogroms will come again. There's no hiding. Only escaping."

I look at the growing pile of boxes. I don't want to leave our home. But then I think of that terrible night: the horses, the shouting, the fire, Mr. Moskowitz. Papa is right. We *do* have to go.

❧ ❧ ❧

It's time to say goodbye to our cottage, the cherry tree whose pink blossoms cover the ground like a carpet every spring, the fence with the gate I loved to swing on. The chicken coop is empty now; Papa sold the chickens at the market. I think of how many times I grumbled about having to take care of them—the smell of the coop, the way they sometimes pecked my hands—and yet when I see the door standing open, with nothing inside, my heart constricts.

The worst is saying goodbye to Mala. Papa

has sold her too, and the new owner is coming to take her away. I hug her neck and press my lips against her muzzle. "I'll miss you," I whisper. The black triangles of her ears prick up as if she understands me.

All morning long, our neighbors—the rabbi, the butcher, and the candlemaker—come quietly to say goodbye. They know it's dangerous to bring too much attention to a Jewish family leaving the shtetl; it's dangerous to bring too much attention to a Jewish family at all.

Papa has hired a wagon to take us to the port. Two big, spotted gray horses with huge heads and large brown eyes are ready to pull it. They seem like good, solid horses, but they are not Mala. Tears fill my eyes, though I try not to let them fall. Still, Sarah sees and comes over to comfort me. "Are you sad about going?" she says, slipping her little hand in mine.

I nod. "Are you?"

"No," she says.

"Why not?" I ask, surprised.

"Because we're going to have fun! A ship! Water! America!"

I do not think this trip is going to be fun. Not one bit. But I say nothing.

Riga, the capital of Latvia, is many *versts* away from our village. We spend four days and four nights in the wagon. Since we have no money for an inn, we sleep by the side of the road, with Mama and Papa taking turns at remaining awake. The horses shift and snort their way through the night.

Gradually, the small shtetls and the forests give way to towns. As we *clip-clop* along, I can see what the war has done: trees scarred by bullet holes, empty trenches, coils of barbed wire.

Soon we come to the grand port city of Riga. It's larger than any town I've ever seen. There are so many people, and they all seem to be in such a hurry. And I've never seen such houses, even bigger and finer than the one where the count lived. I see a cathedral, with a tall black clock tower pointing straight up into the sky, and an enormous palace made of pale orange bricks.

But there is no time to really look. We have to hurry to the waterfront, where the ship is waiting. The dock is filled with noise and confusion—so many people, so many boxes and bags and trunks and valises. We have to stand for hours in a tightly packed line that moves slowly up the gangplank. Finally, we're on board, and the great boat, the SS *Breslau*, begins its long journey across the ocean.

At first, I'm miserable; we all are. The boat rocks and heaves constantly, and we get sick to our stomachs. Mama finds us metal buckets, and we stick close to them, never knowing when the awful waves of seasickness will come again. Gittel and Avram look green; Sarah can't stop moaning. But eventually, the sickness fades, and I begin to look forward to each new day. I love the glittering waves with their lacy tips and above them, the wide open sky. I also love having so much time to whittle. I finish the fish I started back home and go on to carve a gull, a cat, and a rabbit.

One sunny afternoon as I'm sitting on deck whittling, Avram sits down next to me. My first thought is to hide my new animal—an owl— but he's already seen it. So I keep working.

"You're good at this," he says after a while. "Much better than I am. It should have been you in the shop alongside Papa. Not me."

"Do you really think so?" I ask, amazed. He's never expressed admiration for me before, and I realize that it matters to me.

"I really do," says Avram.

"You don't like wood carving, do you?" I ask.

"No," Avram answered. "I don't."

"Why not?" As we talk, my hands seem to move more quickly and confidently. Here is the owl's beak; here are his wide, round eyes.

Avram shrugs. "Papa is disappointed in me."

"Did he say that?" I ask.

"He didn't have to. I can tell."

"That's too bad," I say. I don't like to disappoint Papa either. "If you really don't want to be a woodcarver, you shouldn't have to be one. People should get to do what they want."

"They should," Avram says. "But that doesn't seem to happen much. I don't want to be a carver, and I'm supposed to be one. You want to carve, but you can't. It isn't fair."

"No, it isn't!" I agree. I'm surprised to find that there's comfort in just being heard.

"Maybe it will be different in America," Avram says.

"Maybe," I say. "Maybe not."

Avram turns to go below deck. The sun remains high, so I continue working.

When I look up again, I see Papa standing there. "May I see?"

I hand him the owl.

"It's a bit rough in spots," says Papa. "But basically good. Keep going."

Papa's words make me want to work even harder—to be worthy of his admiration. And I know I can improve, too. I make a promise to myself to whittle every day, even when we arrive in America.

Papa goes back downstairs, and I sit looking at the owl. When I'm finished, I'll give it to Sarah. Maybe it will cheer her up. Unlike the rest of us, Sarah hasn't fully recovered from the seasickness. While the other girls her age run and play along the ship's decks, Sarah sits watching, her eyes not focused on anything in particular.

I know that Mama is worried about her too. I'll finish the owl and give it to her as soon as I can.

But that very night, Sarah suddenly comes down with a fever. The doctor on board the ship comes, but after examining her, he says there's nothing he can do. He tells Mama he will return in the morning, and he leaves.

Sarah remains huddled under her blanket in the cramped cabin we all share. Her eyes are closed; her breath comes in shallow gasps. She shivers as Mama sponges her down with cool water. Mama's face looks so tired.

"I can wash her," I say. "Why don't you take a rest?"

"I can't have you getting sick too," she says. "Go." But before I do, she kisses my forehead quickly. "You're a kind girl."

I go looking for Papa. I find him on deck, near where we had our talk earlier. He's leaning over the ship's railing, staring out at the dark water.

"She's very sick, Papa, isn't she?" I ask.

"Very," says Papa, turning his gaze to me now.

"Will she be all right?"

"I don't know," Papa says.

"Do you think she might die?" It's a terrible question, but I have to ask.

Papa puts his arm around my shoulders and holds me tightly. We don't say anything. Silently, I offer a prayer for my sister. And later, when Papa and I go below deck once more, I work on the owl as if Sarah's getting well depends on it.

The next day Sarah is still shivering with the fever. Her skin turns waxy, and I can see the pale blue veins beneath its surface. The doctor just shakes his head. He can do nothing. Mama looks worn to the bone, and even big, strong Papa seems to have shrunk.

But on the third day, the fever breaks. The shivering stops, and Sarah is able to sit up in bed. She greedily drinks the tea that Mama offers her, holding the cup with two hands. She is thin and weak, but she is alive.

Gittel and I cover her with kisses. Avram scoops her up in his arms and tosses her high. I show her the owl, and she claps her small palms, then reaches for it eagerly.

It's only later that we realize what's changed. She doesn't answer to her name or respond to noises of any kind. When the fever left, it took her hearing along with it.

The doctor returns. He takes his silvery instruments from his black bag and checks her eyes and ears, her nose and throat. Sarah just smiles. The doctor takes out two metal rods and bangs them together. The sound makes me cover my ears. Sarah doesn't even turn her head.

"There's nothing we can do," says the doctor, putting his instruments back in the bag. "You're just lucky you didn't lose her."

"You mean that she'll never be able to hear again?" Mama asks. The doctor shakes his head, and Mama presses her face to Papa's chest. Gittel and Avram hold hands.

I can't look at any of them; instead, I look at Sarah, who is busily making the owl swoop and fly. Up and down, up and down. She is the only one in this cramped room who doesn't seem unhappy. The wooden owl seems to be bringing her so much joy that she doesn't pay attention to any of us. *I'll carve you another owl,* I silently promise my sister. *I'll carve you enough owls to fill a whole forest.*

Chapter 5
Brick

It is September when we arrive at Ellis Island. We pass another island first, the one where Lady Liberty stands, but Mama and Papa don't seem interested in her. They're too worried about other things—like the doctor who examines us and, when he discovers that Sarah is deaf, almost sends her back to Russia. Mama is eaten up with worry. Finally, after poking and prodding every bit of poor frightened Sarah, the doctor decides that she is well and signs the paper that will allow her entry into America.

Then there is our name: Breittelmann. Papa pronounces it slowly and carefully so that the immigration official can write it down correctly.

But the line of people waiting behind us is long, and the official is in hurry.

"Too many letters!" he says impatiently to Papa. "Let's call you Brightman—no, that's still too long. How about Bright? Yes, that'll do."

"But—" begins Papa. It's no use, though. The official calls "Next!" and waves Papa away. Papa gathers his papers, peering down at his new name. Not that he can read the letters anyway; none of us can. "Bright," he says, trying it out softly. He sounds as if he has just lost something, something precious.

From Ellis Island, we travel into New York City. I could not have imagined such a place. So big, so crowded, so noisy. New York City makes Riga look small. I hear people speaking Yiddish, but many people speak American too.

"Not American. English," Papa corrects me.

Everything's so strange to me. No wooden houses, no thatched roofs, no trees, no brooks, no woods. Instead, wherever I look, I see hard surfaces: brick and stone, metal and glass. To me, they seem cold and ugly.

For the first few days, we stay with our cousin

Chana, sleeping on the floor and trying to get used to our new surroundings. Chana helps us find a small apartment on Stanton Street, in a neighborhood full of other immigrants. Many, like us, are from Russia. But others come from Poland, Latvia, Lithuania, or Germany.

The new apartment is up two flights of steep and narrow stairs. The rooms are dark and small; the few windows face the dingy back courtyard. I'm thrilled to have running water—back in Russia, we drew water from a well in a heavy, wooden bucket—but not about sharing the bathroom with the two other families who live on our floor. And I don't like how cut off I feel from the outside; it's down two long flights every time I want a breath of air.

Even worse is that Papa can't find a job carving wood. The shops he hears about are very far away, in places like Connecticut or New Jersey. And they're not interested in hiring a newly arrived Russian Jew who knows only a few English words. Every morning, Papa goes out looking for work, and every evening, he comes back looking discouraged and tired. Finally, he gets a job, but not as a woodcarver. He works at a grocery store, keeping the shelves stocked and helping customers.

Mama gets a job too. She works in a factory where she makes silk flowers, and she takes in sewing for extra money. Gittel can help her, but my sewing isn't good enough. So I offer to iron the mended clothes.

I scorch a delicate cotton nightdress, leaving a dark brown mark on the front that no amount of bleach will remove. I feel terrible. Mama has to pay for the ruined garment. It costs as much as all the money she made from the mending. The worst part is that Mama doesn't even scold me. She just doesn't let me iron again.

To make up for it, I keep Sarah entertained. Now that she understands that she can't hear, this is not an easy job. Sometimes she kicks and yells; other times she cries. I try to soothe her, but it's hard.

The High Holy Days arrive. Our kitchen is too small for Mama to cook for any guests, so we have our *erev* Rosh Hashanah dinner with Chana, the cousin who let us sleep on her floor.

The next day, we go to services at the brick shul on Eldridge Street. It's nice, but I feel out of place. I can't help thinking of our shul back home in Russia. I knew every face on every bench. And I knew every bench too! And every column and the lions at the front and the bimah, because Papa helped carve them all.

I miss our cottage, the shop, the village, and everything we left behind when we crossed the ocean. Why, here in America, I can't even whittle. I used up all the bits of wood I had brought with me on the boat, and I have no way to get more. And even if Papa were able to get me wood, I would have no time anyway. I have to get up early, quickly drink down my tea while it's still hot enough to burn my tongue, and then hurry off to school. After school there are lessons to do at home. Soon it's night, and I climb into bed exhausted, only to start all over the next day.

Back in our village, only the boys went to school, where they studied Torah and prepared for becoming bar mitzvah. I used to be jealous that Avram got to learn while I had to stay home and do chores. Sometimes I would sneak into the schoolroom after the boys had left. I touched the pages with the mysterious squiggles that I knew were words. When Papa found out, he didn't get angry. No, he sat me down beside him and taught me to read.

I love reading almost as much as I love carving, and I used to read the few books we owned—a Bible and a book about talking animals called *Aesop's Fables*—over and over again. So when I first found out I would be going to school, I was happy.

But school is not what I thought it would be. Since we don't speak American—no, English— Gittel and Avram and I are put in a class with very little children, some almost as young as Sarah. Gittel and Avram seem to pick up the language right away and are soon moved to another class. Not me. The new words and new sounds are baffling. I can't say them, understand them, or read them. I was so good at reading in Yiddish—Papa was proud of how quickly I caught on. And Mama always praised the way I expressed myself. But now I'm stuck here with the babies.

The teacher, Miss Flannery, is a kind woman with gold-rimmed glasses and a tidy gray bun. She gives me a book filled with big, colored pictures. A single word is printed below each one. I can't read the words, but I can understand what they must mean from looking at the pictures. *Dog. Ball. House. Pear.* My cheeks burn as I turn the pages. This is a book that would be perfect for Sarah. I'm too old for this book. Can't Miss Flannery see that? Or maybe she thinks that with my too-small dresses and my strange foreign words, I'm so unlike the rest of the girls that I won't mind.

And I *am* unlike them. At recess and at lunch, they ignore me. So I sit alone, chewing on the jam sandwich Mama has packed for me. At the end of the day, I grab my books and hurry home. I would run, but the narrow streets are too clogged with pushcarts and people.

Back in Russia, I had so many friends. But here, I have no one. I beg to be allowed to stay home with Sarah, who spends her days in the apartment, playing with the animals I carved and making pictures on day-old newspapers.

But Mama and Papa say no; here in America, children have to go to school. "Education is a gift, *tochter*," Mama says. "You are a lucky girl." But I don't feel lucky.

I envy Sarah—but also Gittel and Avram, who seem to be adjusting to this new life. Avram has a friend, Max, who's teaching him to play a game called stickball and to ride a bicycle. With her perfect braids and the dresses she has started sewing for herself, Gittel is popular and sought after. All the girls in her class invite her home at lunchtime or after school.

By now, it's winter. There's snow, though not much, and it quickly turns to ugly gray slush. I think of the snow-covered roofs and branches back in Russia. When it snowed, the meadow was covered in white. Often, mine were the first and only tracks to cut across it.

I've grown since we left Russia. I'm now taller than Avram, and my old winter coat no longer fits; my wrists poke out of the sleeves, and the buttons don't close. But Mama is so busy with sewing for other ladies that she doesn't have time to make me a new coat. So I go to school in the old one, with a shawl of Mama's tied over it to keep me warm. I often lag behind, letting Gittel and Avram go ahead. I'm in no hurry to get there.

I make my way through the crowded streets, stopping to stare at the sights along the way. A vendor has posted a sign with a picture of a pickle. Beneath it are some words. I can't read them. But passing the sign day after day, I become familiar with the look of the words, and when I see one of them in a newspaper ad, I say to Mama, "Look. It says pickle." Mama, who can't read it either, asks Avram if that's right. When Avram says yes, I actually laugh out loud. *Pickle*—the first English word I recognize all on my own.

After that, I study the signs even more closely. A shop whose window is crammed with spools of thread, pincushions, and packets of needles has a sign that says *Sewing Supplies*. Another shop that displays petticoats and garters is *Ladies' Undergarments*. Little by little, I teach myself to read the signs. I can read the picture books at school with ease and say the words aloud too, though with a thick accent. But it doesn't matter. I'm reading—and speaking—English.

Soon I'm better at speaking than Mama and Papa and even Gittel and Avram. Now, if someone in the family doesn't understand an English word, I'm the one they ask. How proud that makes me. Miss Flannery suggests that I move ahead to a class with children my age. Finally!

But the best day comes when our class splits into two groups. The girls are going to a room where we will learn to baste, embroider, and sew. The boys are going to something called woodshop. Woodshop! My heart leaps at the sound of the word. I get one of the boys to tell me where the room is, and after school has ended for the day, I go there myself.

I don't know if I'll be allowed to trade sewing for woodshop. In Russia, girls couldn't learn to work with wood. But doesn't Papa always talk about the freedom we have in America? No pogroms, not here. Maybe it will be different with woodworking too.

I look around the room. Tables, benches, and tools. Several saws, stacked planks of wood, and a sandy-haired man—the teacher, I guess—wearing a leather apron. Papa once owned such an apron too, but it's gone now, burned in the fire.

"Did you want something?" asks the teacher pleasantly.

"I want to come to woodshop. Not sewing. Woodshop. To carve."

"Only boys come here," says the teacher. He doesn't sound unkind, only puzzled.

"I know. But I am girl who wants . . . to carve," I say.

"I'm sorry," says the teacher. "No girls. Just boys."

"Oh." I turn away, disappointed. No different than Russia after all. As I walk out the door, my foot brushes something. I look down to see a block of wood.

I kneel to pick it up. It must belong in the woodshop. I should take it back.

But I don't. Instead, my fingers close tightly around the wood. It's the first piece I've held in a long time.

At home, I hide it in the round metal biscuit tin where I keep my treasures—the first tooth

I ever lost, a perfectly round white stone, and a shining, green-blue feather I found while walking in the woods. This little piece of wood is a treasure too, and one day, I'll know what to do with it. Until then, it will be safe in the box.

The day after my talk with the teacher, I ask Avram if he has to go to woodshop.

"I'm supposed to," he says. "All the boys are. But I managed to get out of it."

"How did you do that?" I ask.

"Woodshop is always at the end of the day. I told the teacher that I have a job and need to leave early."

"A job? What job?" I ask. He hasn't mentioned a job before. Do Papa and Mama know?

"I'm making deliveries for a man who sells buttons. Max lets me use his bicycle, and I can get back and forth really fast. Three deliveries a day, sometimes. They pay me ten cents for each, and sometimes there's a tip, too. Think of it, Batya—if I make enough money, I can buy a bicycle of my very own!"

My brother looks so happy. I picture him skipping stones or running, riding a bicycle, hitting a ball. Avram needs to do these things as badly as I need to carve. I shouldn't judge him. Or try to stop him. "I hope you do make enough money," I tell him. "And that you can buy the best bicycle in all of New York."

MITTENDORF & GRAU
Latest, improved CAROUSEL

Chapter 6
Iron

I start skipping school. Not every day. Just once or twice a week. I know it's wrong. But I think of the woodshop and how disappointed I was to be told *no*. Well, skipping school is my own way of saying *no* right back. I have a hunch Avram knows, though he says nothing. I'm grateful for his silence.

I spend my "free" days roaming the neighborhood, making sure I avoid Essex Street, where I might run into Papa. One day, I almost collide with Mama, who is taking a basket of mended clothes to its owner on Hester Street. I realize that I'll have to be more careful.

The next time I skip school, I duck into the

Seward Park Public Library, a red brick building on East Broadway. It's warm, it's free, and best of all, it's crammed with books! I've never seen so many books in one place. I want to read them all.

Reading takes me completely outside of myself. I'm not awkward Batya with the heavy accent and the worn-out clothes. No, when I read, I'm the fine lady in the ermine-trimmed cape, the clever detective who solves the crime, the mermaid who swims beneath the waves. What better escape could anyone want?

One day, a librarian in a starched white blouse and gray flannel skirt asks if I would like to fill out an application for a library card. I shake my head. It's not that I wouldn't like a library card; I'd love one. But I can't risk her asking me questions, like where I live or why I'm not in school. And if Mama or Papa sees me with a book, they'll want to know where I got it. So I now have to avoid the library too.

The next morning, I leave the apartment with Gittel and Avram. Once we get to the street, I tell them, "You go ahead. I'll catch up."

"Slowpoke," says Gittel. "You'll be late."

"So what?" I say.

Gittel shakes her head, and she and Avram walk on. After they've gone, I happen to look down at the street. I see a nickel winking up at me from the sidewalk!

I can buy so many things with a nickel: three bagels, a bag of nuts, candy galore, or five egg creams—a fizzy chocolate drink that I've recently come to love. But I decide to use the nickel as subway fare—to go somewhere else, some other neighborhood.

Even though I know my parents wouldn't approve, I'm going to do it anyway. Mama and Papa don't understand how hard it is for me here. Gittel and Avram have both found a way to belong in this new place. Sarah and I have not. And Sarah is locked into her silent world where it seems harder and harder for me to reach her. I miss her, but what can I do about it? I feel so helpless. So sad.

All the more reason to escape, if only for the day. A pair of glass globes marks the entrance to the subway station on Grand Street. I go down the stairs. My nickel buys a paper ticket that I hand to the ticket chopper. He puts it down the glass chute and turns a crank, and the chopper gobbles up the ticket.

On the platform, I sit down on a bench and wait for a train. A couple of times I get up and look down the dark tunnel to see if it might be coming. But the edge of the platform is scary, and I immediately scoot back to the safety of the bench.

Finally, a train approaches. Oh, the noise it makes when it arrives, thundering into the station like a thousand horses all at once! I cover my ears, but I keep my eyes wide open.

The subway car is painted a dark, glossy red. The seats are wicker-covered and trimmed in the same color.

The doors slide shut behind me, and the train takes off with a little jolt. I grab a pole and hold on tight. We're going so fast. Even Mala's gallop is nowhere near this speed. I walk over to the window and, pressing my hands against it for support, peer out. Glimpses of tunnel, mysterious lights, dark stone walls. There's a whole underground world here, right beneath my feet: trains heading north, south, east, and west. I could stay down here, traveling on one or the other, all day. But I want to see the city above as well as below. So when the train pulls into the next station, I get out.

Once I'm in the street again, I begin walking with no particular direction in mind. Soon, I come to a wide street called Fifth Avenue. How elegant it is! I see women wearing fur coats and matching hats. One wears a beaded cape and carries a parasol of black silk. Holding her arm is a fine gentleman in a dark coat.

I see several long motorcars too: black, cream-colored, or the color of the wine Papa pours on Shabbos. Soon I come to a long, curving stone wall that surrounds a big park. Horses, lined up and harnessed to carriages, wait patiently along the wall. I look past the carriages. Trees! Finally! So this is where they keep them.

I hesitate, unsure if I'm allowed to enter. Maybe it costs money to go inside. But I see people walking in and out. No one charges them admission. So I go in.

Even with the bare trees, the park is lovely. I walk until I get tired and have to sit for a while on a bench. Eventually, I head back out into the street. Where is the subway? I think I can find my way back to it.

Suddenly I realize, with dawning panic, that I don't have a nickel to get home. I'll have to walk. But in which direction?

I look around. I see a lady pushing a baby buggy and a man with a small dog. I decide it's better to approach the lady, though I really would like to pet the dog.

"Excuse me," I say, wishing I didn't have such a strong accent. "Can you tell me how to go to Stanton Street?"

"Stanton Street?" says the woman. "That's way downtown. You can take the subway. It's around the corner."

"I want to walk," I say. Can she tell I'm lying?

"Really?" asks the woman. "It's very far." I feel her studying me, taking in the outgrown coat, the shawl. "Here," she says, suddenly reaching into her purse. "Take this." She gives me a nickel, the price of the fare.

"Are you sure?" I'm half grateful, half ashamed.

"Yes, I'm sure," says the woman.

"Then thank you!" I say. "Thank you so much!"

"I wouldn't like to think of you walking all that way alone," says the woman, glancing at the baby, who's asleep in the buggy. "It's so far."

I hurry down the subway steps. How foolish I was! And how lucky. Next time, I have to remember that I'll need money not only for my trip but to get home as well.

Of course, money is not so easy to get. Papa and Mama have to pay rent as well as buy food and Mama's sewing supplies. There's almost nothing for luxuries, certainly not for subway rides like the one I just took. I know that any money I need I will have to get myself. But how?

Avram has a job delivering buttons. Gittel makes money with her needle. What can I do? Although I ponder this the entire ride, I come to the Grand Street station without an answer.

When I walk into our building and check the mailbox downstairs, I see a letter from the school addressed to Mama and Papa. I pluck it from the batch of mail before anyone else can see it. I have a strong feeling that the letter is about my many absences. I wish I could rip it up, but I don't dare. So instead, I tuck it into my biscuit tin. Mama and Papa will never look in there.

The next day, I go to school. I'm afraid to miss two days in a row.

At home that afternoon, I find Mama in a tizzy. In her lap is a dress made of emerald-green taffeta. All around her lie scraps of black velvet ribbon and dark green lace.

"It's this dress!" she says when I ask what's the matter.

"What's wrong with it?"

"I made a mistake in the hem, and I have to redo it. It's for a fancy lady uptown, and she wants it tonight. But I told Mrs. Feldman I would deliver these clothes too. I won't have time to do both! Can you take them to her?"

"Of course, Mama." I set down my books and pick up the basket.

"Thank you!" Mama says, and she writes down the address.

Mrs. Feldman lives on Rivington Street. It's not far. I find the building and ring the bell. Mrs. Feldman is waiting at the door.

"Right on time," Mrs. Feldman says. She gives me three cents as a tip. I tuck the copper pennies into my pocket, where I can almost feel them glow. Here is my answer! I can make deliveries for Mama and earn tips for my effort.

My plan works out perfectly. Mama appreciates the help, and I appreciate the money. Pretty soon, I have twenty-five cents stashed away in my secret tin. Twenty-five whole cents. Just think of how many rides I can buy with that much money!

But there is something else I want to buy too: colored pencils, colored paper, and a pair of blunt-edged scissors. I teach Sarah to fold the paper and draw the simple outline of a girl on the folded rectangle. Next, I show her how to cut the girl out and unfold the rectangle to reveal a chain of paper dolls, all holding hands. Sarah's face opens into a broad smile. She gestures excitedly to me. I can see that she wants to make more. Soon the floor is covered with chains of paper dolls. I've spent ten of those precious pennies well.

For the next few days, I force myself to go to school, but the following week, I once again convince Gittel and Avram to go on without me. Then I double back in the other direction. In my pocket are fifteen cents—five to take me on a ride to some new and unknown place, and five to bring me safely home again. The final five, I'll spend on candy—sour lemon drops, perhaps, or a red-and-white-striped peppermint stick. Or maybe I'll buy a whole bag of chocolate marshmallow twists: chocolate on the outside and sweet, fluffy filling inside. For the first time, I can see that America is a place of many choices. And right now, some of them are even mine.

Chapter 7
Jewels

I take the train toward a place called Brooklyn, which is at the very tip of the city, bordered by the same ocean we crossed to get here. Now that I've seen the ocean, I have an urge to see it again.

I study the subway map posted in the station. The last stop on the train is Coney Island. Coney Island will be my destination.

It's a long ride, but I don't mind. I have my bag of candy and a newspaper someone left behind on my seat. Slowly, I turn the pages of the paper as I munch on a marshmallow twist. I can read all the words easily now. The train emerges from its underground tunnel onto an elevated track. I put aside the newspaper so that I can look out the window, gazing at the sky, which today is a bleached, wintry blue. I've come to like some things about New York City, but I still miss the open spaces of the country I left behind.

At last, the train reaches the Coney Island station, and I get off. Only one other person is left in the car, a girl with a kerchief tied at her chin. She looks as if she could be from our village, but she walks quickly away before I can be sure. After I've watched her go, I start walking too.

The houses are lower here, and the streets not as crowded. The smell of the sea is tangy and sharp. The wind is sharp too, but I don't mind. In fact, it feels good, whipping through my hair.

Soon I begin to see signs advertising the most astounding things: Ramos the Amazing Sword Swallower, The Bearded Lady, Aaron's Acrobatic Troupe, Jerry's Jugglers. I've stumbled upon an amusement park. It's kind of like the fair, back in Russia, but bigger. I pass a roller coaster and a Ferris wheel. The great machines are silent and still now, but I can almost imagine what it would be like to be here on a summer day.

I come to a round structure that looks like a giant cake. It's all boarded up, but one of the boards is loose. There's a sign near it:

Mittendorf & Grau
Latest, Improved
CAROUSEL
In Operation from April through October
Mermaid Avenue, Brooklyn, New York

No one is around, so I step closer and jiggle the loose piece. It moves easily, letting me peek inside. There, behind the wooden covering, is a ring of the most beautiful carved horses I have ever seen. Horses leaping, horses prancing, horses with their front hooves held high in the air as if they're about to begin a dance. Their wooden tails stream out behind them; their wooden manes rise in wild peaks. They're painted in a rainbow of colors: scarlet, apple green, royal blue, violet, pumpkin, ebony, and dazzling white. Some have real plumes attached to their heads; others have bridles covered with glittering jewels. Some are decorated with carved wooden flowers. There are other animals too: a spotted frog with a waistcoat, a kangaroo, and a zebra. But my eyes keep coming back to the horses.

This carousel is far bigger—and grander—than the one I saw in Russia. These horses belong in an entirely different realm. They are dream horses, made by miracle workers. I have to come back here to see them spin and turn. I have to!

Finally, I turn away. I've eaten all but two of the marshmallow twists, which I'm planning to give to Sarah; I want to see her smile when she takes the first bite. I start to feel a little rumble of hunger, but if I use my remaining five cents for food, I won't be able to get home. Besides, everything around here seems to be closed and shuttered. The wind has picked up, and I'm cold as well as hungry. I should go home.

I see another sign hanging in front of a building.

Mittendorf & Grau
Carousel Works

Mittendorf and Grau—I just saw those names. Through a large plate glass window, I see more than a dozen men wearing leather aprons like the one Papa used to have. Some are standing; some are sitting. Occasionally one will come through the doors and go into a building right next door. I walk straight up to the window to get a better look.

Stacks of crudely carved horse heads stand in one corner. Legs are in another pile, bodies in yet another. I watch, fascinated, as a young man stirs something in a pot. It looks like molasses, dark and sticky. It must be glue, because he uses it to put the pieces of the horse together. He attaches a clamp to hold the glued pieces together and places them on a rack to dry. These are carousel horses!

I'm so absorbed that I barely notice the stout man with the tweed jacket as he hurries by; he brushes so close that he bumps my shoulder.

"Sorry, girlie!" he says in Yiddish. I watch as the man goes into the building next door. I've been so interested in the carving and gluing that

I haven't paid much attention to that building. But now, I follow at a slight distance and walk up to the window.

There are more horses, only not so crude anymore. Their bodies and heads are more finely carved, and each of their faces has a different expression. They're also covered with thick, white paint. Is this the color they're going to be when they are done? I think of the carousel I saw and decide that the answer is no. And when I see one of the workers pick up a sheet of sandpaper and begin rubbing, I know I'm right. Sanding is done before the final staining or painting. I watched Papa and the other workers enough times to know that.

I see a man in a smock dip a brush into a can of chestnut-brown paint and begin applying it to one of the white horses. Next to him are several large, open boxes of fake jewels—blues, reds, pinks, purples. So this is where the horses are painted and decorated before being sent out into the world. I could stand here all day, but the stout man comes out again, and this time, he looks at me more closely.

"You like the painted ponies?" he says, still speaking in Yiddish.

"Oh no!" I answer in English. I don't exactly choose English; the words just pop out. "I don't like them—I *love* them!"

"Well, you've come to the right place," he says, switching to English too. His accent is like mine. "Want to come inside and get warm?"

"Yes, please." I follow him into the workshop.

"I'm Gus," he says. "And you are . . . ?"

"Batya Bright." The new name doesn't sound too bad. In fact, I like the way it sounds. Lively. Fun, even.

The men have stopped for lunch, and food begins emerging from tin pails: hunks of salami, dumplings, pickled herring, rolls, bagels, and slabs of cheese. My stomach rumbles. I still have two marshmallow twists in my pocket, but they're for Sarah, and I'm *not* going to eat them no matter what.

"Hey, fellas, can't you see our guest is hungry?" Gus says. Caught!

"Who's hungry?" says a man with a gold front tooth and a thick mustache. "We can't have that!" He pulls off a piece of his bagel and hands it to me. All the other men contribute small portions of their own food, and soon I'm munching happily.

"So what brings you out here, katzeleh?" asks Gus. *Katzeleh.* That's Papa's nickname for me.

I shrug. And brace myself for what's next.

"Shouldn't you be in school?" asks the man with the gold tooth.

"Watching all of you is better than school!" I say boldly. The men laugh. And to my great relief, they don't ask again.

After the eating is done, a girl comes into the room carrying a teapot. "Sophia!" cries Gus. "Come meet our new friend, Batya."

Sophia smiles, and I recognize her—the girl in the dotted kerchief. "Would you like some tea?" she asks.

I see the other men have brought their own glasses or cups. "I have nothing to drink from."

"I'll get you something." She pours tea for the men and leaves, returning with a cup. "You can use this." The tea is hot and sweet.

When the men return to work, I follow Gus

into the paint shop. He stops in front of a gray horse. The horse's mane and tail are mahogany colored, and his saddle is the color of an eggplant, trimmed with gold. Gus applies a coat of clear, shiny varnish all over the head and body. He works quickly and neatly.

"There." Gus wipes off the brush with a strong-smelling liquid. "Turpentine," he explains, noticing my wrinkled nose. He points to the gray horse. "Now he needs to dry, and then he'll be decorated."

"With those?" I gesture to the gem-filled boxes.

"Yes," says Gus.

I sigh and Gus looks at me again.

"You want to paint, katzeleh?"

"No, to carve!" I blurt out. "I want to carve the horses, the tigers, the rabbits—anything, I don't care! But really, the horses most of all."

"Carve?" says Gus. "Hmm. We do take on apprentices. But they're always boys."

"Boys, boys, boys!" I say. My cheeks feel hot, and I know they're turning pink. In a minute, I might actually start to cry. "That's all I hear!

Boys carve. Girls don't. Why not? My papa is a carver, and I want to be one too!"

I'm worried I've said too much. Gus will be angry, and he'll ask me to leave.

"Your father is a carver? Where does he work?" Gus doesn't sound angry. Only curious.

"Well, he *was* a woodcarver. In Russia. But there was a pogrom in our village. The shop burned down. We had to leave."

"Didn't we all?" Gus's voice is sad.

"Now he works in a grocery store," I say.

"Why don't you tell him about us, katzeleh? The bosses are always looking for good carvers."

"All right," I say. But I know I won't tell. If I do, I'll have to explain about skipping school, the subway rides, and the hidden letter.

Gus walks me to the door. "Come back and see us," he says. "Bring your papa too." I nod and smile, but guilt makes my stomach tighten. How I wish I *could* bring Papa here! He misses being a woodcarver. Not that he ever says as much; even when I asked him, he said, "We do what we have to do, Batya." But I could see the sadness in the set, straight line of his mouth.

The subway train comes almost immediately. When I reach my stop, I head up the stairs. The last light is fading, and the wind feels even sharper. I bury my chilled hands in my pockets. The marshmallow twists are still there. But wait, what's this? I pull out something pink and sparkling: a teardrop jewel. It's one of the fake jewels from the shop. Gus must have slipped it inside when I wasn't looking. I stare, wishing it would offer solutions to my problems. But the trinket just glitters in my palm, and after a moment, I tuck it carefully back in my pocket.

Chapter 8
Silence

Of course I *know* I shouldn't go back to the carousel shop. There are so many reasons: I'll get caught, my parents will be angry, and my teacher will be angry. Still, whenever I manage to get hold of a few nickels' worth of coins, I hop on the train, and off I go.

Lately, the shop has been busy, gearing up for the summer season. Gus and all my other new friends are making horses not only for the carousel in Coney Island but for carousels all over the country. I hear the men name their destinations: Saint Louis, Missouri. Cleveland, Ohio. New Orleans, Louisiana. Saint Paul, Minnesota. Towns in Virginia, Georgia, and even California. Some horses will be used on brand-new carousels. Others will replace horses on existing carousels. Even the most well-carved wood warps and cracks over time, so new horses are always needed somewhere.

Even though I'm not allowed to carve, the men are still grateful for my help. Gus shows me how to prepare the glue. It comes in large, dark squares that look like soap. He teaches me to put a square in the pot and then, when it begins softening, to stir until it starts to boil. Only when it's boiling is it hot enough to use. But it's also dangerous; one day a dot of glue burns my wrist, and although the burn is small, it hurts all day long.

I also sweep the floors and hand the men rags or brushes. And Gus shows me where and how to attach the jewels to the bridles and saddles. I love everything I'm learning, but my fingers itch to carve. Still, I know I ought to be grateful for what I'm allowed to do.

Soon I get to know all the other men in the shop: Vanya and Karl, Fritz and Giuseppe, Marco and Sasha. All these men are immigrants too. They come from Russia, Poland, Germany, and Italy. And I get to know Sophia, who's Vanya's niece.

"Do you want to be a woodcarver?" I ask.

"Heavens, no!" she says. "I want to be a nurse or a teacher. But you have to go to school for those jobs." Sophia is fourteen and doesn't go to school anymore. "You're in school, right?" she asks. I nod. "But you come here instead?" I can tell she finds that puzzling.

"I don't like school," I tell her.

"I would love to go to school," she says wistfully. Too bad she and I can't trade places. Then we'd both be happier.

Sophia tells me it was hard for her to learn English. "Once, I thought *pig* meant dog. I kept calling 'Here, piggy, piggy,' to a dog I wanted to pet. Everyone laughed at me. Or I'd get lost on the subway or bus because I couldn't ask for directions or follow the signs."

I wish I had met her when we first arrived here and I felt so embarrassed to be struggling with the language. It would've been reassuring to know that I wasn't the only one who had trouble.

I feel at home at the shop. The men share their stories and their food, and they're always giving me little things: jewels, feathers, bits of ribbon and leather. I save all of these scraps for Sarah, though I can't give them to her until I can think of a way to explain how I got them. The only men I don't meet are Mr. Mittendorf and Mr. Grau. Gus doesn't think they would like having a girl around the shop, so whenever they come by, I swiftly slip out or hide.

In February, I begin to notice a change in the light. Dusk comes later now, and the five o'clock sky still shows a bit of pale winter sun. And soon enough, spring arrives. How glorious it is! I use two precious nickels to take a ride back to Central Park, where the trees are now covered in delicate green buds. I see a patch of crocuses, some lilies of the valley, and a whole hedge of brilliant, yellow-branched forsythia. And then there are the birds. No chickens, of course. No owls. But scrappy gray and brown sparrows, chattering madly on the sidewalks, and pigeons.

But just as the world seems to be coming to life, Mama gets sick. She can't go to her factory job and can't do any sewing. There are no more tips without Mama's sewing. Even though her head aches and she is coughing, Mama tries to get up, but Papa says no.

"You go back to bed," he says. "The girls will help." Gittel makes soup and bakes bread. I clean and take care of Sarah. Poor Sarah. She grows angrier and angrier in her silent world. She cries for no reason and flings the owl I made across the room. It doesn't break, but there is now a dent on the beak where it was smooth before. She rubs her finger over the damaged spot, tears running down her cheeks. "I'll fix it," I tell her, even though I know she can't hear me. "I'll make it as good as new."

So it's a huge relief when Mama feels well enough to get back to her job and her sewing. Lots of work has piled up, and I'm busy once more, trotting all over the neighborhood making deliveries. When I have four nickels' worth of tips, I decide to celebrate: two nickels for subway fare, and two nickels for candy.

I spend a long time at Mrs. Gottbaum's store on Orchard Street and come home with glittering crystals of rock candy, licorice whips, coconut creams, wintergreen mints, and an orange lollipop, fat and round as a harvest moon. "Here," I say to Sarah. "For you."

But Sarah just looks at it before handing it back. She doesn't even seem angry anymore. She seems defeated, which I feel is much worse. I kiss her on the forehead and tuck the lollipop in my apron pocket for later.

* * *

Armed with my nickels and my candy, I set out the next day. When I get off at the Coney Island subway station, I can see gulls wheeling in the sky, squawking as they hunt for food. At the carousel shop, Gus greets me like an old friend.

"We missed you. Sophia too—she's been asking about you."

The shop is busier than usual. Sophia tells me that there are big orders from far-off cities, and the men have to rush to fill them in time. They carve, they glue, they sand, and they paint. The air is filled with sawdust, and the sound of the tools creates a sweet music. There's a lot for me to do too. At the end of the day, I'm tired but happy. I race to the train, aware that I've stayed later than usual. Well, Mama and Papa are so busy that it's unlikely they'll notice. And even if they do, I suppose I can make up some reason why I was delayed. The thought of lying—again—gives me a pang, but what else can I do? If I tell, I'll never be allowed to return to the shop.

I climb the stairs two at a time, hoping that Mama isn't home yet. But when I open the door, I have a shock. Not only are both Mama and Papa at home, but they're sitting at the table with Miss Flannery.

"Hello, Batya," says Miss Flannery. "It's good to see you."

"H–h–hello," I stammer.

"Batya, Miss Flannery say you no go to school. True, this?" Mama's English has improved, but her words sometimes still come out in the wrong order.

"Well . . ." I'm more ashamed than I would have thought possible.

"We sent letters home . . ." continues Miss Flannery.

"Letters?" asks Papa.

I just look at the worn floorboards, wishing I could disappear beneath them.

"Batya?" Miss Flannery prompts.

"I have the letters," I say miserably. "I'll get them." I fetch the tin and hand the letters to my mother.

"Let me," Miss Flannery says. She opens the letters and reads them aloud. There's a long silence when she has finished.

"Miss Flannery," Papa says at last. "Our Batya, she good girl. We must let her say what happen."

"Yes," agrees Mama. "Batya must say."

"Well, I, uh, you see, at first, it was just because of the woodshop. I wanted to go so much, but they wouldn't let me, and—"

Suddenly there's a loud crash, followed by the sound of wailing. Mama jumps up, and Papa follows. Miss Flannery and I remain at the table. But I can't look at her, and so I look down at my scuffed black shoes with their peeling leather and cracked toes.

When Mama and Papa reappear, Mama is leading Sarah by the hand. Sarah hangs back, her face red and tear-streaked. She must have had another fit of temper.

"I sorry," Mama says. "This Sarah. I can no help. Get so angry."

"Hello Sarah," Miss Flannery says gently. "It's nice to meet you."

"She not hear you," Papa says tapping his ear for emphasis. "No work."

"You mean she's deaf?" Miss Flannery asks.

"Yes," I say. "She got a fever on the boat. She hasn't been able to hear since then."

"I see," says Miss Flannery. "I want to know more about that. Much more. But first, I want to hear what you have to say, Batya. About why you've been missing school."

So I go back to my story, shy at first. But soon it all comes tumbling out—my frustration about not being allowed to work with wood and my discovery of the carousel shop.

"Batya was wrong to lie," says Papa sternly. This is the worst part of all—disappointing Papa. But his next words are an utter surprise. "The carving. How bad our Batya need to carve." He pauses, thinking. "Batya, show teacher." I must look puzzled so he switches to Yiddish. "Get the animals you made. I want her to see them."

I leave the room and return with all the animals I've carved: the owl with his dented beak, the fish, the kitten, the rabbit, the bear . . . and I add one more, taken from my pocket. It's the head of a horse, carved from the bit of wood I found at school. I wished I could have carved an entire horse, but the piece of wood wasn't big enough. I think it's the best thing I've ever done.

Miss Flannery looks at the animals, running her fingertips over their carved surfaces, inspecting the smallest details. "These are wonderful. Simply wonderful," she says.

I smile. Whatever else happens, at least Miss Flannery understands. Papa smiles too. Even though I was wrong to lie, he's still proud of me.

"I'd like to show these to the woodshop teacher," Miss Flannery says. "And the principal. When they see them, I know that they'll make an exception and let you take woodshop. You have my word."

Woodshop at school! Can it be?

"There's one more thing, though," says Miss Flannery. She sounds serious, and I see the anxious looks Mama and Papa exchange. "I'd like you to bring Sarah to the school for an evaluation."

"An evaluation?" I ask.

"Yes," says Miss Flannery. "To see if she can learn to speak with her fingers. Sign language. Though she may never be able to hear again, she may be able to communicate like that." She brings her face close to Sarah's. Sarah backs away slightly and clutches the damaged owl tightly.

"It's hard to live in silence, isn't it?" she says to Sarah. "No wonder you're so angry. But I think we can help you, Sarah. I hope you'll let us try."

I hold my breath. Will Sarah hit her? Throw something? But no, Sarah just looks steadily at Miss Flannery. After a moment, she reaches out and touches the teacher's kind face.

Chapter 9
Music

Thanks to Miss Flannery, Sarah starts going to school right along with us. She attends a special class for children like her. None of them can hear, but all of them can learn. Soon Sarah is "talking" with her fingers, signing words like *hungry, thirsty,* and *sleepy.* I've attended some of the classes so I can learn the signs and teach them to the rest of the family. Now that Sarah is able to communicate with us, she is much happier.

Meanwhile, Mama gets a new job—at a dressmaker's shop uptown, on Twenty-Third Street. She says it's much nicer than working in the factory, and the owner, Mrs. Wadjenska, gives Mama leftover fabric. Mama is able to make us each two new spring dresses. One of mine is a red-and-black plaid. The other is blue with white buttons.

I feel so grown up and, yes, even ladylike in the new garments. The first time I wear the blue dress, Gittel tells me how nice I look. The compliment makes me try harder with my appearance. I polish my shoes. I keep my apron clean and pressed. And I get what I think is a brilliant idea. But it's not something I can do by myself. I need help. So I ask Gittel.

"You want me to *what*?" she fairly shrieks.

"You're always telling me how messy my hair is. And you're right. But it's so hard to keep it tidy. So if you cut it, right to here—" I put my hand to the bottoms of my ears, "it'll look neat all day long. Please, please, *please,* won't you do it?"

"Mama won't like it," she says, but I can tell she is thinking it over.

"Blame it on me!"

"All right," she grumbles. "But you'd better stay still."

I sit down and barely even breathe. Gittel

moves around me, scissors in hand. She takes the job very seriously, measuring with a comb, tilting my chin this way and that, snipping all the while. Soon the floor is littered with hair. Finally, she sets the scissors down. "Take a look."

I pick up the hand mirror. Is that poised, grown-up-looking girl really me? My hair is shining, neat and smooth, curling just the slightest bit beneath my ears.

"You know, I thought it was going to look dreadful," Gittel says. "But I was wrong. Batya, you look beautiful!" Gittel has never given me so much praise in her whole life. I jump up and fling my arms around her. She hugs me back.

And that's how Mama finds us when she comes through the door. She's shocked, but I explain my reasons as I sweep the snipped hair, and she calms down.

"It's pretty," she says at last. She turns to Gittel. "You did a good job." Gittel and I both beam. And I decide to make Gittel a sewing box where she can keep her supplies. It'll be a surprise.

Best of all, I take Papa to the carousel shop, where he does some sample carving and is hired on the spot. He buys new tools and a new leather apron. Now that he's carving again, he wants Avram to become an apprentice. "The boss will make a place for you," Papa says. "You'll learn to carve horses."

"No time," says Avram. "I have to go to school."

"School is almost over for the year," Papa points out. "You'll have the whole summer."

"Papa," Avram says, "I don't *want* to become a carver. Not of carousels or anything else."

"Why not? It's a fine trade."

"But not the trade I want, Papa," Avram says. His tone is respectful but firm.

"I don't understand," Papa says.

Mama sighs. "Things are different here," she tells him. "You have to let him make his own way."

I think of the shiny blue bicycle Avram has bought with his very own money. Now he can pedal around the neighborhood making even more deliveries.

Papa looks from Avram to Mama and back with a lost look on his face. "I just always thought

I would pass it down, the way your grandfather passed it down to me."

"Why can't Batya become an apprentice?" Avram asks.

"Girls can't be apprentices," says Papa.

"That was back in the old country," Avram points out. "Maybe it's different here. Everything else is."

I pray that he's right.

I have to go to school now, so I can't spend long days at the carousel shop anymore. But I am finally allowed to attend woodshop, just as Miss Flannery promised.

I'm the only girl in the class. The boys tease me about doing boys' work.

Once, I yell at them, trying to make them stop. They only tease me more.

At home, I confide in Avram.

"Ignore them," he says.

"Ignore them?" What kind of advice is that?

"It's only fun to tease someone if there's a reaction. But if you ignore them, it's no fun for them anymore."

"Really?"

"I'm a boy, right? So I know how boys think." He gets up, and I notice how he's grown. Avram says he's a boy, but soon he'll be a man.

The next time I go to woodshop and Iggy Rothstein starts chanting the usual taunts, I look right through him, as if he's a pane of glass. Iggy isn't used to being ignored, so he tries again. "Batya likes to do what *boys* do."

"Iggy!" says the teacher sternly. "Behave yourself!" Flustered, Iggy goes back to work.

Later, Iggy comes over to me again. I tense, waiting for the teasing to start. But Iggy just watches as I sand the piece of wood in my hands. He doesn't say a word. I feel uncomfortable, but I keep my eyes down and continue to work.

"That yours?" Iggy said at last. I nod.

"Well, it's not too bad," he says gruffly. "Actually, it's pretty good." He walks away.

"Thank you," I call out after him. Although he doesn't turn around, I know he's heard me.

A few days later in class, Iggy asks me for help with his birdhouse.

At recess the next day, he runs up to me and taps my shoulder. "Tag!" he calls. "You're it!"

I grin as I dart off after Iggy. I'm fast, and it doesn't take me long to catch him. *"You're it!"*

After this, the boys include me in all their games. And the girls do too. Now, I start looking forward to school and am actually sorry when the term ends.

June again. So much has happened since last year!

As a treat, Papa takes us all out to Coney Island. This is the first time I've been to the amusement park after dark, when what seem like a thousand brilliant lights flood the night sky. And we're going to the carousel! After all the months of working in the shop, I feel I have a claim to it. It belongs, in part, to me.

Along the way, Papa buys us ears of roasted corn and apples that have been dipped in red candy. But I'm impatient to get to the carousel. Soon, we hear the lively music—calliope, cymbals, drums—and there we are, right in front of it.

How splendid it is, spinning like a top, horses rising and falling as if they're dancing. It's even better than I imagined when I stood here in the cold, peering in through the loosened slat of wood.

"Did you make any of those horses?" Gittel asks Papa.

"No," Papa says, smiling down at her. "But next summer, you'll see my horses. They replace a few every year."

"*I* helped with some of them," I add.

"You!" Gittel is surprised. "I knew you were going to woodshop instead of sewing. And I know about all the animals you carve. But I didn't know you knew how to make great big carousel horses!"

"Well, I still have a lot to learn," I say. "I didn't do any carving. I just helped decorate them."

"Which ones?"

"You see that brown horse? With the lilac saddle?" Gittel nods. "I did his harness and his bridle. The jewels too."

"He looks very grand," Gittel says.

"And that white one? I did her bridle and saddle. And a little bit of her ears—the man who was doing them was sick, so I finished up."

"You did a wonderful job." So now Gittel is praising my work along with my haircut. I puff up with pride.

"And when Batya's finished with that wood-shop class, I bet she'll be ready to carve one of those horses from start to finish," says Avram. He puts his arm around my shoulders and gives me a hug.

First, a compliment from my oh-so-perfect sister, and now a hug from my brother—what else will this day bring?

"Anyone want a ride?" asks Papa.

So we all get on, even Mama and Papa. I choose the white horse. To me, she is perfect. The horse circles once, twice—and the third time, I lean over, just past her proudly arched neck, and I catch the brass ring.

Later, Avram rides the roller coaster, which is too scary for me, and after that, we all take turns shooting darts at a target. I'm not very good at darts, but Avram wins a glass rooster that he gives to Sarah. Riding home, Gittel and Sarah fall asleep, and even Avram dozes lightly. I'm tired too but remain awake, replaying the evening in my mind. The carousel ride was the best part.

I look down at my hands, the hands that still long to carve, and that's how I see the rooster slipping from Sarah's loosened fingers. I catch it before it can fall to the floor and break. I think of the chickens back at our cottage, but the memory seems distant now, and it no longer makes me ache. I cup the rooster carefully in my hands, determined to keep it safe for Sarah.

Chapter 10
Ash

Over the summer, we still have chores, but at least now I can whittle again. Papa brings me wood from the carousel shop. But these bits and pieces no longer satisfy me. I've learned to handle larger, more serious tools, like a saw and a gouge. My hands need more than the little whittling knife can offer.

I'll just have to wait until school starts in September. Although Miss Flannery won't be my teacher, she made sure I'd be allowed to take woodshop again. I've already made a shelf that I gave to Mama, who declared it was perfect for her spices. Next, I'm going to start on that sewing box for Gittel.

We meet some other kids in the neighborhood and play tag, hide-and-seek, and hopscotch. We blow bubbles using wire loops and a flat pan of soapy water. Avram teaches us to play stickball. Gittel and I don't like it at all, but Sarah does. Who would have thought that such a little girl could hit a ball so hard or run so fast? If it rains, we stay inside and draw or make paper dolls.

One morning late in July, I'm washing the breakfast dishes. Avram is out making a delivery on his bicycle, and Mama has gone uptown to the dress shop. Gittel is out with Sarah, and Papa is at the table with his coffee and the Yiddish newspaper. Mama still drinks tea made in the samovar we brought from Russia. But Papa has switched to coffee.

Today I'm planning a trip to the library; I've started going again. The librarian even remembered me. "I'm glad you came back," she said. "Are you sure you wouldn't like to fill out the papers so you can have a library card?"

This time, I agreed, and now I lug books back and forth from East Broadway to our apartment. I was excited when I came across a biography of Helen Keller. Like Sarah, Helen lost her hearing from a fever. *And* she lost her eyesight. Like Sarah, she was angry for a long time. But then a wonderful teacher—sort of like Miss Flannery—named Anne Sullivan helped her. Helen was able go to school and then to college! Now she leads a happy, full life even though she can't see or hear. This book gives me so much hope. I've read it twice, and I want to read it to Mama and Papa.

All of a sudden, I hear a strange sound. "No!" Papa bursts out, pushing the paper away. It falls to the floor, and the pages fan out at his feet.

"What's wrong?" I ask.

"A fire late last night! In Coney Island! There was so much damage . . ."

"Not the carousel shop?"

"Not the shop. But so many of the rides— and the carousel! Gone!"

Images fill my mind. Fires, jugglers, stampeding horses, Mr. Moskowitz. I burst into sobs.

Papa gathers me in his arms. "I'm sorry I scared you. I wasn't thinking."

"I thought we left Russia to get away from all that! But it's followed us here!"

"What?" says Papa, looking confused. After a moment, though, he understands. "No, *katzeleh*. It wasn't like that."

"Are you sure?"

"Yes," says Papa. "It was an accident. Just a horrible accident." I must look unconvinced because he adds, "No one was hurt."

"No one?" I ask.

"No one," Papa says firmly. "The amusement park and the carousel were closed for the night. Everyone was gone."

"How did it start?"

"The police will investigate. But you know how easy it is for wood to catch fire."

I do. There are tin pails filled with sand at the carousel shop. Sand, Gus explained, can smother a fire. But if this fire started at night, there was no one to dump sand onto the flames.

"What happened is very sad," Papa says, refolding the paper. "But it will be fixed. You'll see." He glances at the clock. "I have to go to work now."

"Please, Papa, let me come with you!"

Papa hesitates. Is he thinking about the terrible morning after the pogrom? "All right. But you'll have to hurry."

The ride seems to take forever. Usually, I love it when the train emerges from underground and I can look out the windows. But today, I barely notice, and I fret every time the train makes a stop. Finally, we pull into the last station. I'm so impatient that I jump out of my seat and race down the steps. Papa rushes to keep up.

First, we go to see the carousel. We can't get too close because the police have put up ropes to keep people back. We can see chunks of charred wood and piles of ash. I can make out a few horses that haven't been completely destroyed. But not many.

"Let's go," Papa says. "They'll need me at the shop."

When we arrive, we see Gus holding a clipboard. He looks down at it as he barks orders to the men swarming around. Papa quickly joins them. I remain off to the side. No one notices me, not even Sophia, who is there too.

Suddenly the activity stops. I wonder why

until I see the man in the linen suit and crisp shirt. Mr. Mittendorf. I've seen him before, though I always made sure he didn't see me.

The workers gather around him. "The carousel suffered terrible damage in last night's fire," he begins. "We're grateful no one was hurt. But the carousel is ruined, and we've lost all the horses we had scheduled to ship out. And here we are at the height of the summer season, gentlemen. The absolute height." He takes a handkerchief from his pocket and pats his face. "That means we'll have to double our production schedule. The shop will be open for extended hours, and there'll be two shifts. If any of you know any carvers in need of work, have them see me right away."

"Excuse me," I amaze myself by saying. I'm so nervous that my voice comes out squeaky and high. No one hears me. So I try again. "Excuse me, Mr. Mittendorf. Would you let me help?"

He swivels around sharply. "*Who*," he demands, "are *you*?" His angry stare is frightening, but I stay where I am and stare straight back at him.

"I'm Batya Bright," I say. I still speak with an accent, but I no longer mind. The accent is part of who I am. "That's my father. Over there." I point to Papa.

"Well, Batya, thanks for your offer. But the answer is no. We've never had girls as apprentices before. Only boys."

"Why can't girls be apprentices?" I don't know where my courage comes from. "I'm good at carving, Mr. Mittendorf. If you'll only—"

"I'm sorry," says Mr. Mittendorf. "I'm a busy man. Now will you excuse me?"

"Mr. Mittendorf, I speak, please?" Papa steps forward. He has taken off his cap and twists it in his hands. "My Batya, she is good carver. Everyone say so. And you need help, Mr. Mittendorf."

But Mr. Mittendorf is not convinced. "No girls," he says. "That's final."

He turns again to the crowd of men. "I want everyone in the paint shop." The men shuffle out. Papa lags behind, squeezing my shoulder as he passes.

"We tried, didn't we?" he says softly.

"You would make a good carver, I know you would," adds Sophia.

I nod and remain where I am. After all the activity, the shop seems very quiet now. I look around; there are several roughly carved horse heads sitting on the floor. I've watched how heads like these are finished many times. I've stood by as Vanya or Marco used the tools to shape the features and bring the animal's face to life.

Suddenly, I have an idea that makes my heart pound. The horses need to be finished. And I need to carve. Gus showed me how the carvers work from wooden models called prototypes. Well, there's a prototype right here. I can follow it.

But the heads are heavy. I can't lift one by myself.

I see one on a worktable. It seems as if it's waiting for me, begging me to finish it.

I'm scared but ready. Everything I've done so far—watching Papa, carving my own animals, working here and at school—has prepared me. So what if I'm scared? I pick up a gouge, look at the wooden prototype, and begin.

As I work, my hands almost feel as if they don't belong to me. They're so sure. So confident. I know how to apply the right amount of pressure here, to chip away at some excess wood there.

It's hard work. I have to use all my strength, not just in my hands but in my arms and shoulders too. My face and my body grow damp. But I don't stop.

After a while, I've carved one of the almond-shaped eyes, and then the other. Next, I move down, toward the lips, curving back over the teeth. They're difficult to get right, but I keep working, glancing at the wooden prototype every so often. If I just take away a little more here and round it a little bit more there . . .

An image of Mala comes into my mind. How eager she was when she saw the lump of sugar, how her nostrils flared and her eyes widened when Papa tried to shoe her, the way she twisted her head and arched her neck. Mala! I still miss her, but I know that she wouldn't be happy here in the city with the cobbled streets, the noise, and the crowds. Her spirit is in me, though. And it guides me as I work.

"*What are you doing?*" asks a stern and unfamiliar voice.

Startled, I look up. There stands a man in a pea-green suit and a black-banded straw hat—Mr. Grau, the carousel company's other owner.

"I'm carving this head." I try to keep my voice steady.

"How dare you! That head is very costly. You'll ruin it."

"I know it's costly, sir," I say. "My father works here. He's a carver. I'm a carver too. Look." I point to the work I've done—the proudly flared nostrils, the lips, the beginning of the tongue.

"*You* did *this?*" Mr. Grau leans closer.

"Yes, sir," I say. "I'd never spoil one of your fine horses. If I didn't know how to carve, I wouldn't touch it."

"You did all this?" Mr. Grau repeats, more to himself than to me. "Why, this is quite good. Quite good indeed." He looks over at me. "Who did you say you were?"

"Batya Bright." I look at the horse. It seems to me that even though she isn't finished, she is looking right back at me, giving me courage.

At that moment, Mr. Mittendorf reappears. When he sees me, his expression darkens.

"Why are you still here?" he demands. "You should be waiting for your father outside."

"George," says Mr. Grau, "just look at this."

"What?" says Mr. Mittendorf angrily. "Has she actually been touching our horses? With tools? I'll have her father fired at once!"

"George!" interrupts Mr. Grau. "Stop yelling for a minute and have a look, would you?"

Mr. Mittendorf stops talking but is still frowning as he inspects the horse's head. He looks at it from every angle, and after that, he runs his fingers over it for good measure. "Is it possible?" he murmurs.

Mr. Grau says, "That's what I wondered too. But she's good—she really is. And we need every pair of good hands we can get right now."

"You're right about that," Mr. Mittendorf says grimly. "You!" he calls to me. "Come here."

"Yes, sir?" I'm trembling.

"Would you like to be an apprentice for the rest of the summer?"

Would I *like* that? Haven't I hoped and dreamed, practiced and waited for this chance? "Yes, I would."

"It will be a lot of work," he continues. "The schedule will be busy. You'll have to come in early and stay late, do what you're told, and not question anything. Can you do all that?"

I lived through a pogrom, I left my home and sailed across the ocean, I learned to speak and read a new language, I taught myself to carve and found a way to learn the other skills I needed, so yes, I think I can do that.

I answer with a simple "Yes."

"Then you can come in for the summer to learn and to work with your father. Even if you *are* a girl."

Yes, I'm a girl, I think proudly. *A girl who can carve as well as any boy, better than my big brother, almost as well as my papa. I'm Batya, and I'm not just the woodcarver's daughter anymore. I'm Batya, the woodcarver. Just you wait and see.*

Author's Note

I have always loved carousels, and I clearly remember the carousel in Brooklyn's Prospect Park, where I took my earliest rides. The great, leaping horses frightened as well as transfixed me; at first, I would only sit with my father on the high-backed stationary bench—painted deep red and trimmed in gold—as the merry-go-round whirled and spun. Gradually, I worked up the courage to sit on a stationary horse, my father waving from the sidelines, and then, one memorable day, I sat astride a leaping white horse all by myself. I can still taste the triumph I felt.

I've continued to love carousels, and even when I no longer wanted to ride them, I always took the opportunity to see a new one in any town or city I visited. I liked to see the differences in style, the variation within the form. My own children rode the carousels in Prospect Park, Central Park, and Coney Island; they too were carousel lovers. But it was only recently that I learned about the connection between

European-born carousel carvers—expert crafts-
men who made a home in America—and my
own Russian Jewish roots.

Many of the Jewish woodcarvers from
eastern Europe—men who had helped decorate
their shuls with lions, arks, and bimahs—were
forced by widespread persecution and anti-
Semitism to leave their homes and adapt their
talents to the new land in which they found
themselves. An exhibit at New York City's
American Folk Art Museum charted this
journey, demonstrating how the skills learned
in service to God were used toward entirely
different ends in America.

The show identified the work of individ-
ual carvers, pointing out their particular sty-
listic trademarks. But there were no women
carvers, and a small note explained that this
was because girls were not allowed to join the
woodworkers' guild.

In that one offhand comment, I had found
the kernel of a story. What if there had been a
girl who wanted to carve? What would she have
done? That ambitious girl became Batya. I tried

to imagine a situation in which a girl would have been exposed to the life of a carver but prevented from taking up that life herself because of the rules and conventions of her time. But I also wanted to imagine a solution to the problem, a creative way for her to overcome the obstacles through a combination of courage, perseverance, and talent.

My maternal grandmother, Tania Brightman, was born in Ekaterinoslav, Russia, in the early part of the 20th century. She lived through numerous pogroms and the Russian Revolution. After her father was killed, her mother took her and three of her siblings on the long journey to America. Like Batya and her family, they boarded a ship in Riga. And my grandfather Morris Brightman—also Russian-born and reared—was a woodcarver. Although never a professional, he loved to work with wood, and his garage woodshop, littered with sawdust, crammed with his tools and his many projects, was steeped in his passion. The parallels between their lives and Batya's end there. But these are the biographical threads that I used to weave my own tale. If fiction can be described as the charmed intersection of the real and the imagined, then I hope that in telling Batya's story, I have done credit to both.

Timeline

1817: The Connecticut Asylum for the Education and Instruction of Deaf and Dumb Persons opens. Students study a system of communication that later becomes known as American Sign Language.

1867: Frederick Savage creates the modern carousel with horses that go up and down.

1880: Helen Adams Keller is born in Tuscumbia, Alabama. At the age of nineteen months, she loses her hearing and her sight due to an illness. She never regains them.

1880–1914: A large wave of Jewish immigrants arrives in the United States from eastern Europe.

1880–1920: These decades are known as the golden age of carousels in America.

1885: The Statue of Liberty arrives in New York Harbor on June 19. It is a gift of friendship from the people of France to the people of the United States.

1897: William Morrison and John C. Wharton, candymakers from Nashville, Tennessee, invent cotton candy.

1903: Luna Park, an amusement area in Coney Island, opens. Fires frequently ravage the area. Coney Island suffers major fires in 1903, 1907, 1908, and 1911.

1904: The first underground line of the New York City subway opens on October 27.

1914: World War I breaks out in Europe.

1917: The Russian Revolution begins.

1918: World War I ends.

Glossary

bimah: the platform in the synagogue from which the Torah is read

blini: thin Russian pancakes

challah: a bread eaten on the Jewish Sabbath and on major Jewish holidays

cheder: a traditional elementary school for boys, teaching the basics of Judaism and the Hebrew language

erev: Yiddish for "evening"

katzeleh: Yiddish for "little cat," a term of endearment

kopeck: an old Russian coin, about the value of a penny

pierogi: Russian dumplings stuffed with meat, cheese, or other fillings

pogrom: a form of violent riot or mob attack, either approved or condoned by the government, directed against a particular group. Jews were the targets of pogroms in eastern Europe well into the 20th century.

shtetl: Yiddish for "village"

shul: a Jewish house of worship

tochter: Yiddish for "daughter"

Torah: the first of three parts of the Hebrew Bible. The Torah is divided into five parts, or books.

verst: an obsolete Russian unit of length. It is defined as being 3,500 feet, which is about two-thirds of a mile.

About the Author

Yona Zeldis McDonough was born in Hadera, Israel, and raised in Brooklyn, New York. Educated at Vassar College and Columbia University, she is the author of eight novels for adults and 30 books for children. Her short fiction, essays, and articles have appeared in many national and literary publications. She is the fiction editor of *Lilith*, a feminist Jewish magazine.